A Bed for the Wind

By Roger B. Goodman
Illustrated by Kimberly Bulcken Root

Simon and Schuster Books for Young Readers, Published by Simon & Schuster Inc., New York

10 9 8 7 6 5 4 3 2 1
10 9 8 7 6 5 4 3 2 1 (Pbk)
Library of Congress Cataloging-in-Publication Data   Goodman, Roger B. A bed for the wind/Roger B. Goodman, illustrated by Kimberly
Bulken Root. Summary: A child takes a magical flight through the evening sky looking for a place for the wind to rest. [1. Winds—Fiction.
2. Flight—Fiction.]   I. Root, Kimberly Bulcken, ill.   II. Title   PZ7.G6143Be   1988   [E]—dc19   87-22875
ISBN 0-671-66117-5   ISBN 0-671-69443-X (Pbk)

To Laura
R. B. G.

To the memory of my father
K. B. R.

PETER SAT ON HIS BED. In a moment Mommy and Daddy would be in to kiss him goodnight. While he waited, he thought of many things.

He thought about his baby brother David, asleep in his old blue crib. He thought about the sparrow in the tree outside his bedroom window, and the nest with two brown speckled eggs in it.

One thing puzzled him. On many nights, in the fall and spring when he was getting ready for bed, he would hear the wind. "Who-oo-oo" it would hum sadly as it came down the street. "Who-oo-oo."

"Where does the wind sleep?" Peter asked his mother.

"I'm not sure, darling, but settle down now. Goodnight."

Peter then asked his father. "Where does the wind sleep at night?"

"I don't know, Peter. Why don't you ask the wind?" his father replied as he turned out the light.

In the light from the streetlamp Peter looked at Jumbo. "Do you think I should ask the wind?" The elephant nodded his head in agreement.

Through the window he saw the trees begin to sway. The leaves at the tip ends of the branches started dancing. The wind was not far away. Sure enough, Peter heard the soft "Who-oo-oo" as the wind swung around the corner, level with the window.

"Hi there, Mr. Wind," called Peter. "Hello!"

"Whoooosh!" cried the wind. "Who's calling me?" Peter could just make out the wind's face amidst the thick woolly whiskers that were blowing in every direction.

"I'm up here," said Peter. "And I'd like to ask you a very important question. Please, would you wait just a moment?"

"Surely," laughed the wind, his brown button eyes twinkling.

The wind stirred up four small whorls of leaves and twigs to make a seat for himself.

"Now, how can I help?"

"Well," said Peter, "I was wondering where you went to sleep at night. At bedtime I hear you whistling in the street. You sound so sad."

The wind was silent. Not a leaf stirred.

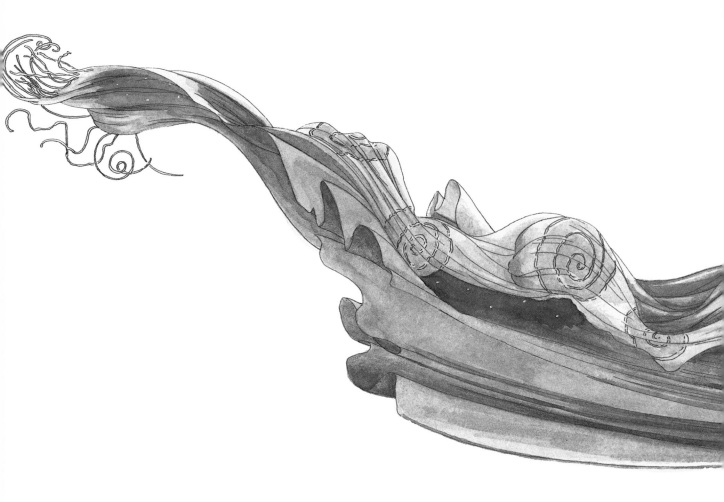

"That's just it," said the wind finally, a tear falling on his whiskered cheek. "I have no place to lie. Whoo-oo—I do get mighty weary. If I were to find a soft and cozy spot, I'd be so happy."

"Well," Peter said, a little cautiously and holding Jumbo tight, "We'd like to help you, if that's all right."

And so it was that Peter and Jumbo were soon astride the wind's back, soaring high above the city.

Peter marveled at the river, curled like a shiny ribbon on a birthday package. He saw the straight avenues criss-crossing like a gameboard and the automobiles like colorful checkers. The sleeping buildings reached up to touch them as they flew over.

"I can see why you can't sleep here," called Peter. "Those buildings would stick like pins—that could hurt."

As they flew on Peter studied the landscape below. The wind was so busy whistling "Whoo-oo," that he didn't look at all.

Peter looked down, first on one side, then on the other. Then he saw it. It was round and blue and shiny. It seemed to be smooth, too.

"Down there," shouted Peter to the wind, pointing to the blue circle. "That could be a good place."

"All right," the wind replied, "Here we go." Very slowly, the wind circled lower and lower.

"It's a big lake," cried Peter. "That should be smooth enough, and not too hard. Be careful," he warned. "There may be rocks!"

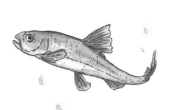

The wind closed his eyes and stretched himself out on top of the water. "Whooo-oof! Ooh!" he thundered. And he leaped away from the lake.

"What's the matter, Mr. Wind?" asked Peter, holding on tight. "Wasn't it smooth and soft enough?"

"Oh, yes it was. But it was also cold and wet. Brrr-oof!"

Off they soared again.

Soon Peter noticed that Jumbo was pointing his trunk towards the ground. He looked carefully. "Yes," he called. "There's a good place."

And down they came again. This time the wind made a smooth glide. He came right down into a long, dry valley. And he snuggled close and lay very still.

"It looks all right," said Peter. "Now how does it feel?"

"Well," sighed the wind. "It's dry and warm. But it's quite a squeeze. I'm too big for this bed."

They passed over a range of steep rocky mountains. There was no sense trying there.

As they were gliding down the other side, the land became soft and green for miles and miles. The wind turned his head toward Peter. "Shall we try that?"

Down they went, slowly and gently. It was a great forest. The tops of the trees barely moved. "This could be it," murmured Peter with excitement. "I think we've found it."

But once again, the wind hurled them into the air. This time the wind was laughing. Laughing so hard, in fact, that his whiskers were wet with tears.

"What's so funny?" inquired Peter, holding tight to the wind's back. "Why are you laughing?"

"Oh, ho, ho, ho," roared the wind. "Whoo-oh-oh, those trees. They tickled my belly! Ah, how they tickled me!"

The wind's laughter sounded like distant thunder as he flew on.

Peter was beginning to feel a little sad and sleepy. They had come a long way, and seen many different places. But they had not been able to find a comfortable bed for the wind. And Peter wanted so much to help his new friend.

"Let's try further west, Mr. Wind," Peter urged. "I think I know a place."

"Here we go," replied the wind, "Into the setting sun."

There beneath them was a large, smooth, flat plain. He looked very, very carefully. There didn't seem to be any hills. No trees grew here. And there was definitely no water in sight.

"This is it," whispered Peter.

"I hope so," answered the wind, by now quite tired.

Gradually they descended, and finally settled gently on the plain. The wind stretched himself out. "Hmmm-mm," he whispered...

"Weary am I, with a safe place to lie..." And before Peter could say anything, the wind had fallen fast asleep.

Peter must have fallen asleep too. Because when he opened his eyes, he was back in his own room, in his soft, warm bed. He pushed back the covers and tip-toed to the window. All was quiet and still. There was no sound of the wind.

But just below Peter's room,
clearly visible in the light of the streetlamp,
were four small whorls of leaves and twigs.

THE END